Birds
of HEAVEN

BY THE SAME AUTHOR

Flowers and Shadows
The Landscapes Within
Incidents at the Shrine
Stars of the New Curfew
The Famished Road
An African Elegy
Songs of Enchantment
Astonishing the Gods

Birds
of HEAVEN

Ben Okri

A Phoenix Paperback

First published in Great Britain
by Phoenix

A division of Orion Books Ltd
Orion House, 5 Upper St Martin's Lane,
London WC2H 9EA

A CIP record for this book is available
from the British Library

ISBN 1 85799 593 7

Typeset at Selwood Systems,
Midsomer Norton
Printed in Great Britain by
Clays Ltd, St. Ives plc

Contents

Beyond Words

I

Aphorisms and Fragments

15

Birds of Heaven

Beyond Words

A Secular Sermon

We began before words, and we will end beyond them.

It sometimes seems to me that our days are poisoned with too many words. Words said and not meant. Words said *and* meant. Words divorced from feeling. Wounding words. Words that conceal. Words that reduce. Dead words.

If only words were a kind of fluid that collects in the ears, if only they turned into the visible chemical equivalent of their true value, an acid, or something curative – then we might be more careful. Words do collect in us anyway. They collect in the blood, in the soul, and either transform or poison people's lives. Bitter or thoughtless words poured into the ears of the young have blighted many lives in advance. We all know people whose unhappy lives twist on a set of words uttered to them on a certain unforgotten day at school, in childhood, or at university.

We seem to think that words aren't things. A bump on the head may pass away, but a cutting remark grows with the mind. But then it is possible that we know all too well the awesome power of words – which is why we use them with such deadly and accurate cruelty.

We are all wounded inside in some way or other. We all carry unhappiness within us for some reason or other. Which is why we need a little gentleness and healing from one another. Healing in words, and healing beyond words. Like gestures. Warm gestures. Like friendship, which will always be a mystery. Like a smile, which someone described as the shortest distance between two people.

Yes, the highest things are beyond words.

That is probably why all art aspires to the condition of wordlessness. When literature works on you, it does so in silence, in your dreams, in your wordless moments. Good words enter you and become moods, become the quiet fabric of your being. Like music, like painting, literature too wants to transcend its primary condition and become something higher. Art wants to move into silence, into the emotional and spiritual conditions of the world. Statues become melodies, melodies become yearnings, yearnings become actions.

When things fall into words they usually descend. Words have an earthly gravity. But the best things in us are those that escape the gravity of our deaths. Art wants to pass into

life, to lift it; art wants to enchant, to transform, to make life more meaningful or bearable
in its own small and mysterious way. The
greatest art was probably born from a profound and terrible silence – a silence out of
which the deepest enigmas of our lives cry:
Why are we here? What is the point of it all?
How can we know peace and live in joy? Why
be born in order to die? Why this difficult one-
way journey between the two mysteries?

Out of the wonder and agony of being come
these cries and questions and the endless
stream of words with which to order human
life and quieten the human heart in the midst
of our living and our distress.

The ages have been inundated with vast
oceans of words. We have been virtually
drowned in them. Words pour at us from every
angle or corner. They have not brought under-
standing, or peace, or healing, or a sense of

self-mastery, nor has the ocean of words given us the feeling that, at least in terms of tranquillity, the human spirit is getting better.

At best our cry for meaning, for serenity, is answered by a greater silence, the silence that makes us seek higher reconciliation.

I think we need more of the wordless in our lives. We need more stillness, more of a sense of wonder, a feeling for the mystery of life. We need more love, more silence, more deep listening, more deep giving.

2

When the angels of the Bible spoke to human beings, did they speak in words? I don't think so. I think the angels said nothing, but they were heard in the purest silence of the human spirit, and were understood beyond words.

On a more human scale there are many things beyond.

A mother watches her child leave home. Her heart is still. Her eyes are full of tears and prayer. That is beyond.

An old man with wrinkled hands is carrying his grandchild. With startled eyes the baby regards his grandfather. The old man, with the knowledge of Time's sadness in his heart, and with love in his eyes, looks down at the child. The meeting of their eyes. That is beyond.

A famous writer, feeling his life coming to an end, writes these words: 'My soul looks back and wonders – just how I got over'.

A young woman, standing on a shore, looks out into an immense azure sea rimmed with the silver line of the horizon. She looks out into the obscure heart of destiny, and is over-whelmed by a feeling both dark and oddly joyful. She may be thinking something like this: 'My soul looks forward and wonders – just how am I going to get across.' That is beyond.

3

A flamenco dancer, lurking under a shadow, prepares for the terror of her dance. Somebody has wounded her in words, alluding to the fact that she has no fire, or *duende*. She knows she has to dance her way past her limitations, and that this may destroy her forever. She has to fail, or she has to die. I want to dwell for a little while on this dancer because, though a very secular example, she speaks very well for the power of human transcendence. I want you to imagine this frail woman. I want you to see her in deep shadow, and fear. When the music starts she begins her dance, with ritual slowness. Then she stamps out the dampness from her soul. Then she stamps fire into her loins. She takes on a strange enchanted glow. With a dark tragic rage, shouting, she hurls her hungers, her doubts, her terrors, and her secular prayer for more light into the spaces around her. All fire and fate, she spins her enigma around us, and pulls us into the awesome risk of her dance.

She is taking herself apart before our sceptical gaze.

She is disintegrating, shouting and stamping and dissolving the boundaries of her body. Soon she becomes a wild unknown force, glowing in her death, dancing from her wound, dying in her dance.

And when she stops – strangely gigantic in her new fiery stature – she is like one who has survived the most dangerous journey of all. I can see her now as she stands shining in celebration of her own death. In the silence that follows, no one moves. The fact is that she has destroyed us all.

Why do I dwell on this dancer? I dwell on her because she represents for me the courage to go beyond ourselves. While she danced she became the dream of the freest and most creative people we had always wanted to be, in whatever it is we do. She was the sea we never ran away to, the spirit of wordless self-overcoming we never quite embrace. She destroyed us because we knew in our hearts that rarely do we rise to the higher challenges in our lives, or our work, or our humanity. She destroyed us because rarely do we love our tasks and our lives enough to die and thus be reborn into the divine gift of our hidden genius. We seldom try for that beautiful greatness brooding in the mystery of our blood.

You can say in her own way, and in that moment, that she too was a dancer to God.

That spirit of the leap into the unknown, that joyful giving of the self's powers, that wisdom of going beyond in order to arrive here – that too is beyond words.

All art is a prayer for spiritual strength. If we could be pure dancers in spirit we would never be afraid to love, and we would love with strength and wisdom. We would not be afraid of speech, and we would be serene with silence. We would learn to live beyond words, among the highest things. We wouldn't need words. Our smile, our silences would be sufficient. Our creations and the beauty of our functions would be enough. Our giving would be our perpetual gift.

4

The greatest inspiration, the most sublime ideas of living that have come down to humanity come from a higher realm, a happier realm, a place of pure dreams, a heaven of blessed notions. Ideas and infinite possibilities dwell there in absolute tranquillity.

Before these ideas came to us they were pure, they were silent, and their life-giving possibilities were splendid. But when they come to our earthly realm they acquire weight and words. They become less.

The sweetest notions, ideas of universal love and justice, love for one another, or intuitions of joyful creation, these are all perfect in their heavenly existences. Any artist will tell you that ideas are happier in the heaven of their conception than on the earth of their realisation.

We should return to pure contemplation, to sweet meditation, to the peace of silent loving, the serenity of deep faith, to the stillness of deep waters. We should sit still in our deep selves and dream good new things for humanity. We should try and make those dreams real. We should keep trying to raise higher the conditions and possibilities of this world. Then maybe one day, after much striving, we might well begin to create a world justice and a new light on this earth that could inspire a ten-second silence of wonder – even in heaven.

Aphorisms and Fragments

From 'The Joys of Story-telling'

1

To poison a nation, poison its stories. A demoralised nation tells demoralised stories to itself. Beware of the story-tellers who are not fully conscious of the importance of their gifts, and who are irresponsible in the application of their art: they could unwittingly help along the psychic destruction of their people.

2

The parables of Jesus are more powerful and persuasive than his miracles.

3

Stories are as ubiquitous as water or air, and as essential. There is not a single person who is not touched by the silent presence of stories.

4

A people are as healthy and confident as the stories they tell themselves. Sick story-tellers can make their nations sick. And sick nations make for sick story-tellers.

5

Great leaders understand the power of the stories they project to their people. They understand that stories can change an age, turn an era round.

6

Great eras are eras in which great stories are lived and told.

7

Great leaders tell their nations fictions that alter their perceptions. Napoleon exemplified this, and made himself into an enthralling story. Even bad leaders know the power of negative stories.

8

All the great religions, all the great prophets, found it necessary to spread their message through stories, fables, parables. The Bible is one of the world's greatest fountains of fiction and dream.

9

The miracles of Jesus came down to us as stories, magical stories. It is the stories, rather than the facts, which still enchant us towards belief.

10

Alexander the Great conquered all of the known world. But Alexander himself was gently conquered by Homer.

11

Without fighting, stories have won over more people than all the great wars put together.

12

The greatest religions convert the world through stories.

13

A great challenge for our age, and future ages: To do for story-telling what Joyce did for language – to take it to the highest levels of enchantment and magic; to impact into story infinite richness and convergences; to make story flow with serenity, with eternity.

14

Stories are the secret reservoir of values: change the stories individuals or nations live by and tell themselves, and you change the individuals and nations.

15

Nations and peoples are largely the stories they feed themselves. If they tell themselves stories that are lies, they will suffer the future consequences of those lies. If they tell themselves stories that face their own truths, they will free their histories for future flowerings.

16

There is a natural justice to the incontrovertible logic of the way stories reveal their hidden selves.

17

Stories are either dangerous or liberating because they are a kind of destiny.

18

The fact of story-telling hints at a fundamental human unease, hints at human imperfection. Where there is perfection there is no story to tell.

19

In the beginning there were no stories.

20

That previous fragment is a story.

21

The universe began as a story.

When we have made an experience or a chaos into a story we have transformed it, made sense of it, transmuted experience, domesticated the chaos.

When we started telling stories we gave our lives a new dimension: the dimension of meaning – apprehension – comprehension.

Only those who have lived, suffered, thought deeply, loved profoundly, known joy and the tragic penumbra of things tell truly wonderful stories.

Stories do not belong to eternity. They belong to time. And out of time they grow. And it is through lives that we touch the bedrock of suffering and the fire of the soul; it is through lives, and in time, that stories – re-lived and re-dreamed – become timeless.

26

The greatest stories are those that resonate our beginnings and intuit our endings (our mysterious origins and our numinous destinies), and dissolve them both into one.

27

Homo fabula: we are story-telling beings.

28

We are part human, part stories.

29

It is through the fictions and stories we tell ourselves and others that we live the life, hide from it, harmonise it, canalise it, have a relationship with it, shape it, accept it, are broken by it, redeem it, or flow with the life.

30

Without stories we would go mad. Life would lose its moorings or lose its orientations. Even in silence we are living out stories.

31

Stories can drive you mad.

32

Stories can heal profound sicknesses of the spirit.

33

It is through their stories that the ancient Greeks so profoundly influence and shape the world. Prometheus, Ixion, Sisyphus, Perseus, the Gorgon's head, Calypso, Odysseus – their stories are eternal metaphors of the partially revealed nature of the human condition.

34
Africa breathes stories.

35
In Africa everything is a story, everything is a repository of stories. Spiders, the wind, a leaf, a tree, the moon, silence, a glance, a mysterious old man, an owl at midnight, a sign, a white stone on a branch, a single yellow bird of omen, an inexplicable death, an unprompted laughter, an egg by the river, are all impregnated with stories. In Africa things are stories, they store stories, and they yield stories at the right moment of dreaming, when we are open to the secret side of objects and moods.

Africa is a land bristling with too many stories and moods. This over-abundance of stories, this pollulation, is a sort of chaos. A land of too many stories is a land that doesn't necessarily learn from its stories. It should trade some of its stories for clarity. Stories hint both at failure and celebration. Dying lands breed stories in the air like corpses breed worms. A land beginning to define itself, to create beauty and order from its own chaos, moves from having too many moods and stories in the air to having clear structures, silences, clear music, muted and measured celebrations, lucid breezes, freed breathing, tentative joys, the limpid freshness of new dawns over places sighted across the sea for the first time. If suffering breeds stories, then the transformation of suffering into a higher order and beauty and functionality breathes tranquillity.

37

Tranquillity is the resolution of the tensions and paradoxes of story into something beyond story: into stillness.

38

Unhappy lands prefer utopian stories.
Happy lands prefer unhappy stories.

39

The stories of the Egyptians and the Greeks, rather than their poems, shaped the world's consciousness and named the stars.

40

For Africans the world is imbued with stories, legends, tales.

41

The African mind is essentially abstract, and their story-telling is essentially philosophical.

42

The happiness of Africa is in its nostalgia for the future, and its dreams of a golden age.

43

In Africa the mood in its music is a poignant golden story of everlasting hope and prayer.

44

Where stories are, struggles have been lived through, fates have been lived out, triumphs have danced with failures, and human destinies have left their imprints and their souls and their stories on the land, in the air, and even on the waters. Strangers to these lands can feel the vibrations of the people's forgotten histories and fates in the air.

45

Moods are stories unspoken, condensed in the air, untold. Stories become moods, and are moods unfurled, allowed to grow.

46

The transparency of excellent stories: words dissolve words, and only things stand in their place.

47

In bad stories words cancel themselves out, and nothing is left. The words return to their source; they desert the page; only meaningless marks are left behind.

48

Story is paradox.

49

The superiority of one writer to another is not just in the quality of language; but also in the quality of the story and the story-telling; the quality of enchantment; and the timelessness of that enchantment. It is therefore futile to speak of superiorities. There is only that which lives, and which keeps on living.

50

Creating the smallest living thing, creating life, no matter how small, is greater than creating a vast dead planet. A thing that lives is a universe.

51

It is in the creation of story, the lifting of story

into the realms of art, it is in this that the higher realms of creativity reside.

52

A good story keeps on growing. A good story never dies.

53

Stories are the wisest surviving parts of a people's stupidities or failings.

54

A people without stories would be a perfected people or a forgetful people, or an insane people – which is to say that they are a mythical people, or have ceased to exist, or are on their way to doing so.

55

Stories can destroy civilisations, can win wars,

can lose them, can conquer hearts by the millions, can transform enemies into friends, can help the sick towards healing, can sow the seeds of the creation of empires, can undo them, can re-shape the psychic mould of a people, can re-mould the political and spiritual temper of an age.

56

Stories can be either bacteria or light: they can infect a system, or illuminate a world.

57

Like water, stories are much taken for granted. They are seemingly ordinary and neutral, but are one of humanity's most powerful weapons for good or evil.

58

It is easy to forget how mysterious and mighty stories are. They do their work in silence, invisibly. They work with all the internal materials of the mind and self. They become part of you while changing you. Beware the stories you read or tell: subtly, at night, beneath the waters of consciousness, they are altering your world.

59

Stories are one of the highest and most invisible forms of human creativity.

60

Stories are always a form of resistance.

61

There is a perpetual creativity involved in story-telling. Stories make people more creative, negatively or positively.

62

The writing of stories: the hidden frame, the hidden harmony.

63

The miracle of stories, and the mystery.

64

The story-telling quality in Mozart's music. How certain bars, certain notes in the Piano Concerto 27 hint at a story that goes something like this: 'One day, when I was happy, a nightingale flew past my window, and the love of my life left me for another.'

65

Music and stories: the notes that haunt us because they have become the moods of our joys and our sweet sadnesses forever.

66

The grief of Orpheus is a story told with anguish over and over again, every day, for seven years, and told in all its agonising internal permutations.

67

Orpheus's grief is the mother of music, but is itself born of story, a story unbearable to live, obsessive to tell – the story of our inescapable loss, and the measure of our love.

68

The infinite interpretability of great stories – and their serenity.

69

To see the madness and yet walk a perfect silver line.

70

The greatest guide is the clearest spirit and mind.

71

That's what the true story-teller should be: a great guide, a clear mind, who can walk a silver line in hell or madness. Dante chose Virgil. I would choose Jesus, or the Buddha, or Lao Tsu, or Homer.

72

Great story-tellers seldom found religions. Great founders of religions are always excellent story-tellers.

73

Only a profound story-teller would say something like: 'Suffer the little children to come unto me.'

74

The great essays on story-telling are done in stories themselves.

75

The true story-teller suffers the chaos and the madness, the nightmare – resolves it all, sees clearly, and guides you surely through the fragmentation and the shifting world.

76

I am not referring to just any story, but only to those great ones, rich and rare, that haunt, that elude, that tantalise, that have the effect of poignant melodies lodged deep in barely reachable places of the spirit. The human race is not blessed with many stories of this quality.

77

The magician and the evangelist have much in common: both have to distract (our attention).

78

The magician and the politician also have much in common: they both have to draw our attention away from what they are really doing.

79

Magic distracts our attention from the hidden methods, art draws our attention to the hidden revelation.

80

Magic becomes art when it has nothing to hide.

81

The higher the artist, the fewer the gestures.

82

The fewer the tools, the greater the imagination.

83

The greater the will, the greater the secret failure.

84

It is precisely in a broken age that we need mystery and a re-awakened sense of wonder: need them in order to be whole again.

85

Philosophy is most powerful when it resolves into story. But story is amplified in power by the presence of philosophy.

86

The infinite life of a beautiful story.

87

Creativity is a secular infinity.

88

Creativity is evidence of the transhuman.

89

Creativity is the highest civilising faculty.

90

Love is the greatest creativity of them all, and the most blessed.

91

Creativity of any valuable kind is one of the fullest expressions of the human and the godlike within us.

The greatest joy is that of love – loving life, loving others, loving yourself, loving your work. The next greatest joy is the freedom to serve.

Creativity is love, a very high kind of love.

The imagination is one of the highest gifts we have.

To find life in myth, and myth in life.

Maybe there are only three kinds of stories: the stories we live, the stories we tell, and the higher stories that help our souls fly up towards the greater light.

97

All great stories are enigmas.

98

Humility is the watchword at creativity's gate.

99

Creativity is a form of prayer, and the expression of a profound gratitude for being alive.

100

Ah, the sweet suffering of creativity.

101

Politics is the art of the possible; creativity is the art of the impossible.

ON KLEE

So you too were on the journey
To the East
Where mystery
Is the stuff of the feast.

Music and nature served you well
Grateful and free, you wove your spell.
You find infinity in small spaces
And magic in the most likely places.

Not for you the loud gesture
The striking death or newsworthy posture.
Wisdom reigns in hidden symmetry
And colours are but charmed invisibility.

What lingers in the soul
Often bypasses the eye
And the birds of heaven, without wings –
How much more sublimely do they fly.

'Beyond Words' was first delivered at Trinity College Chapel, Cambridge, in June 1993

'The Joys of Storytelling' was first delivered at the Cambridge Union, June 1993

Published by Phoenix Paperbacks
in April 1996

Astonishing the Gods

Ben Okri

From the Booker Prize-winning author of *The Famished Road*, comes a playful and bewitching novel which carries the reader to the shore of an enchanted island, a strange but never unfamiliar world where allusions and illusions dazzle, provoke, elude and delight.

This is a story told for a child, set in a time and place familiar to readers of fairytales and myths shot throughout with the magic of Ben Okri's uniquely imaginative prose. It is a myth for our time, a fable about who we are now and how our search for identity affects our perceptions and actions.

ISBN 1 857 99374 8

£5.99

Phoenix 60p Paperbacks

History/Biography/Travel
The Empire of Rome A.D. 98–190 *Edward Gibbon*
The Prince *Machiavelli*
The Alan Clark Diaries: Thatcher's Fall *Alan Clark*
Churchill: Embattled Hero *Andrew Roberts*
The French Revolution *E.J. Hobsbawm*
Voyage Around the Horn *Joshua Slocum*
The Great Fire of London *Samuel Pepys*
Utopia *Thomas More*
The Holocaust *Paul Johnson*
Tolstoy and History *Isaiah Berlin*

Science and Philosophy
A Guide to Happiness *Epicurus*
Natural Selection *Charles Darwin*
Science, Mind & Cosmos *John Brockman, ed.*
Zarathustra *Friedrich Nietzsche*
God's Utility Function *Richard Dawkins*
Human Origins *Richard Leakey*
Sophie's World: The Greek Philosophers *Jostein Gaarder*
The Rights of Woman *Mary Wollstonecraft*
The Communist Manifesto *Karl Marx & Friedrich Engels*
Birds of Heaven *Ben Okri*

Fiction
Riot at Misri Mandi *Vikram Seth*
The Time Machine *H. G. Wells*
Love in the Night *F. Scott Fitzgerald*

The Murders in the Rue Morgue *Edgar Allan Poe*
The Necklace *Guy de Maupassant*
You Touched Me *D. H. Lawrence*
The Mabinogion *Anon*
Mowgli's Brothers *Rudyard Kipling*
Shancarrig *Maeve Binchy*
A Voyage to Lilliput *Jonathan Swift*

POETRY

Songs of Innocence and Experience *William Blake*
The Eve of Saint Agnes *John Keats*
High Waving Heather *The Brontes*
Sailing to Byzantium *W. B. Yeats*
I Sing the Body Electric *Walt Whitman*
The Ancient Mariner *Samuel Taylor Coleridge*
Intimations of Immortality *William Wordsworth*
Palgrave's Golden Treasury of Love Poems *Francis Palgrave*
Goblin Market *Christina Rossetti*
Fern Hill *Dylan Thomas*

LITERATURE OF PASSION

Don Juan *Lord Byron*
From Bed to Bed *Catullus*
Satyricon *Petronius*
Love Poems *John Donne*
Portrait of a Marriage *Nigel Nicolson*
The Ballad of Reading Gaol *Oscar Wilde*
Love Sonnets *William Shakespeare*
Fanny Hill *John Cleland*
The Sexual Labyrinth (for women) *Alina Reyes*
Close Encounters (for men) *Alina Reyes*